INVASION OF THE GIANT NITS

For Herbie, Autumn and the tortoise
- GPJ

To Andy & Jackie, thanks for all the support
- SM

STRIPES PUBLISHING
An imprint of the Little Tiger Group
1 Coda Studios, 189 Munster Road,
London SW6 6AW

A paperback original
First published in Great Britain in 2018

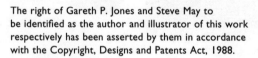

ISBN: 978-1-84715-952-6

A CIP catalogue record for this book is available
from the British Library.

Printed and bound in the UK.

10 9 8 7 6 5 4 3 2 1

GARETH P. JONES

ILLUSTRATED BY

STEVE MAY

stripes

PET DEFENDERS

Protecting those who protect us

Did you know that Earth is under constant alien attack?

Don't worry.

We are the Pet Defenders, a secret society of domestic animals. We are your dogs, cats, rabbits and rodents. While you are off at school or work or doing whatever it is you humans do, we are keeping the Earth safe.

We keep our work hidden because we know what humans are like. The first sight of a Quasar Mouse or a piece of stinky alien cheese and you'll panic.

Before you know it, you'll have blown up the very planet we're trying to defend.

Just carry on as normal — stroke your cats, take your dogs for walks and clean out your hamster cages. Don't forget to feed us, but please ... let *us* take care of the aliens.

Now that you know all this, we need you to forget it. Our specially trained seagulls will take care of that. Ah, here they are with the Forget-Me-Plop now...

SSSPLAT!

CHAPTER 1

❧

PAUSING PHILIP

Mitzy snuggled into the blanket and gave a satisfied purr. Biskit growled and shifted over to make room.

Their owner, Philip, reached down to give them both a little stroke. "Who said dogs and cats don't get on?" he said, sinking his hand into the huge bucket of popcorn.

As he pulled it out, a few pieces dropped down. Biskit moved his head to try and grab one but Mitzy was too fast for him.

"Hey," said Biskit. "I invited you to share

my home. You could share some popcorn."

"You snooze you lose," replied Mitzy.

"I wasn't snoozing. I was watching the film," said Biskit. "And this is a good bit. Danger Dog's about to catch a flaming arrow in his teeth, then snap it in half and send it back to Evil Kitty Cisco."

Mitzy watched as the dog on the screen did exactly what Biskit had just described.

"You have to admit it's a good film," said Biskit.

"It would be a lot better if someone didn't keep telling me what's about to happen," said Mitzy pointedly. "And why do the baddies always have to be cats?"

"They aren't. Not always," muttered Biskit. "In *Danger Dog Barks Back* the baddie is a rat."

"Never a dog, is it?" said Mitzy. "Also, how's he flying that helicopter on his own?"

"He's Danger Dog," said Biskit. "He was trained by the CIA, the FBI, the KGB, MI5 and a secret tribe of Shaolin monkeys in a remote temple in China."

"Biskit, you're a top agent working for a secret agency dedicated to keeping the Earth safe from alien attack, can *you* fly a helicopter?" asked Mitzy.

"I'd give it a good go," said Biskit. He latched his paws around Philip's knees and waggled them as though he were steering a helicopter.

Philip laughed and jumped up, tipping over his bucket of popcorn and spilling the contents all over the floor. "Hey, that tickles. Stop it. What are you two doing? Oh, I see your game. Trying to steal my popcorn, are you?"

Biskit and Mitzy were quick to take advantage of the situation. They ran around hoovering up the fallen popcorn.

On the TV, Danger Dog had jumped out
of the helicopter moments before it exploded
and was parachuting towards the shark-
infested ocean.

"Actually, *this* is the best bit," barked Biskit.

"Hey, stop your barking," said Philip.
"Danger Dog is about to surf on the back of a
shark."

"He's as bad as you are, giving away what's
going to happen," said Mitzy, but she had lost
interest in the film. She was determined to get

as much popcorn as she could before Philip swept it up. Having spent the past few months living on the streets of Nothington-on-Sea she had not yet shaken off the feeling that every meal could be her last.

Philip and Biskit watched open-mouthed as Danger Dog landed on a shark's back. He steadied himself on his back legs, before grabbing the fin and surfing on the shark. A helicopter exploded and the adverts came on.

"And now for a word from our sponsors," said a voice. "Yapp Snax, the pet food that won't ruin your pet's appetite."

"Oh, great, I love this advert," said Philip.

The television showed a chorus line of French poodles and Persian cats wearing tutus, floppy hats and big feather boas. They were high-kicking and waving their paws in the air. It was all done with CGI effects but that didn't bother Biskit or Philip.

"I can do that too." Biskit jumped up on his hind legs while Philip joined in with the singing animals.

"Give your dogs and cats a treat,
With Yapp Snax every day to eat
Our tasty bites are just sublime
They're fabulous and SO divine."

"Woof woof," barked Biskit along with the poodles. "Oh, you missed it," he said to Mitzy.

She stared back at him in disbelief.

"What?" said Biskit.

"You said 'woof woof'," said Mitzy. "I mean, I know it all sounds like 'woof woof' to humans but you actually said it."

"Those are the words of the song. It's so catchy. I love it," said Biskit. "Hey, why are you staring like that?"

"Biskit, look," said Mitzy.

Biskit spun round to discover that the picture on the TV had frozen.

"Philip must have paused it," he said.

"Then who's paused Philip?" asked Mitzy.

Philip was standing absolutely still. He had been in the middle of a dance move so his body was at an extremely awkward angle. But he didn't wobble. He didn't even blink. It was as though he had been frozen in time.

CHAPTER 2

ZED'S MISSION

"Hello, Biskit," said a low female voice. "Good day, Mitzy."

The Pet Defenders turned to see a bulbous-eyed goldfish swimming in the centre of a sphere of clear liquid. With no bowl to contain it, droplets of water splashed out as the fish waggled its tail and moved mysteriously through the room. This was no ordinary fish. It was Barb, an alien who lived in a fishbowl in a vet's surgery and helped out the Pet Defenders when they needed it. She drifted over to the TV.

"Sorry about interrupting your film," she said. "Have you got to the part where Danger Dog jumps off a train and lands in a pit of deadly snakes? That's my favourite bit."

"What are you doing here, Barb?" asked Biskit.

"I am in many places," she replied. "I am a multi-dimensional being. This fish form is simply how I appear in your funny little corner of this galaxy. My understanding of the universe is so beyond yours it would be like trying to explain mathematics to a Momping Mono-browed Stoopida." As she spoke an image appeared of a large alien with small eyes, long hair and a single long eyebrow.

"And they almost went extinct after the entire species forgot how to eat." The voice that said this belonged to a black cat, who stepped out from behind the sofa. The cat wore a collar covered in flashing lights, while on its tail was a high-tech gun and a pendant that looked like a red Button.

"Zed," said Mitzy.

"Actually, it's Senior SUPA Agent Zed now," said the black cat. "I got promoted for arresting those Atomic Burps."

"After we caught them, you mean?" said Mitzy.

"Yes. Champ and I are very grateful for what

you did," said Zed.

"Is Champ here?" asked Biskit excitedly.

"Sorry," said Zed. "You know the rules. He was your partner once but he works for us now. SUPA agents aren't allowed back on their home planets."

"So why are you here?" asked Mitzy.

"I need your help." Zed sprang up on to the arm of the sofa.

"Our help?" said Mitzy. "The last time you were here you said that we were a bunch of petty-minded pets protecting our own little planet."

Zed straightened his legs and arched his back, enjoying the stretch. He dug his claws into the fabric of the sofa. "That's still true but you proved to me that you were the best at what you do."

"What do you want?" asked Mitzy suspiciously.

"Like I said, I need your help. One of our top technicians has betrayed us and we believe she's hiding out on your planet."

"Why don't you use one of your SUPA agents to track her down?" asked Biskit.

"Because Annascratch knows them all, their strengths and their weaknesses, but she doesn't know you," said Zed.

"Annascratch?" said Mitzy.

"Anitch Annascratch, a Tarangutan from the Arachnovian Quadrant," said Barb. The goldfish blinked and an image appeared of a huge spider with eight chunky legs covered in matted orange hair. She walked on her six back legs, freeing up her two front limbs, which she used like arms.

"So she's a big hairy spider," said Biskit. "So what's the problem? Webs?"

"Well, she does have quite powerful webs, yes, but that's not really the issue," said Zed.

"Annascratch is our top technician. She's a gadget genius. She invented the Unmistaker and the Stare Ray that all our agents use. Only now she's turned bad and we need to stop her."

"Stop her from doing what?" asked Mitzy. "Why is she here?"

"Because this planet may be small and insignificant but it is positioned in a spot where the fabric of the universe is particularly thin," said Zed.

"That's why so many portals appear here," said Barb. "It's why you have all these alien invasions."

"I'd hardly call one hairy spider an invasion," said Biskit.

"Annascratch is not working alone," said Zed. "She has an army."

"What kind of army?" asked Mitzy.

"They're called Nano Inventive Trained Soldiers," said Zed.

Barb swished her tail and the image of the hairy spider was replaced by one of a big-bottomed insect standing on its two back legs. Its skin was almost transparent and it had a pair of small pincers next to its mouth.

"*Nano* because they are so small that they cannot be detected. *Inventive* because they are able to use their surroundings to create weapons and—"

"Let me guess," interrupted Biskit. "*Trained Soldiers* because they have been trained as soldiers."

"Yes. These nits have been bred and mutated to become a deadly army. They know every tactic. They can make any weapon with their bare claws. They are undefeatable."

"You say they're small," said Mitzy. "How small?"

"About the size of a speck of dust," said Zed.

Biskit laughed. "Ooh, scary."

"At that size you're right. Unfortunately, Annascratch has run off with her latest invention."

The image moved in on Annascratch's head to show that she was wearing a visor above her eyes.

"It's called a Relativisor," said Zed. "It fires

out a beam that can shrink things down to atomic level or grow them to the size of planets. We believe she is planning to use it to grow an army of Giant Nits."

"And you want us to stop her?" said Biskit.

"Yes. But you're not going to be able to do it on your own. You'll need this." Zed lowered his tail and carefully removed the pendant he was wearing, then he placed it on the carpet with the button pointing up.

"What is it?" said Biskit, sniffing the object.

"Careful. It's a secret weapon," said Zed. "And I would like Mitzy to wear it."

"Why me?" asked Mitzy.

"You know what they say, if you want something done quickly, get a dog. If you want something done properly, ask a cat," said Zed.

Biskit let out a small growl and Zed jumped up on to the back of the sofa and took a couple of steps along it.

"You're asking us to take a piece of alien technology and use it without having any idea about what it will do?" said Mitzy.

"Yes." Zed hopped to the windowsill. "I trusted you. Now you need to trust me."

Mitzy looked into his green eyes, smiled, then slipped her head through the chain so that the button hung under her chin.

"We won't need your gadgets," said Biskit with a low, determined growl. "Whatever she's planning we'll stop her."

"That's the spirit," said Zed. "Do your thing, jump about and bark, fetch a stick then, when you need help, press the button." Zed slunk around the room. He took a close look at the TV screen, then tried a piece of popcorn. "Ew. Salty," he said before nudging a button on his collar and vanishing in a flash of light.

Barb drifted over to the window. "Yes, good luck," she said. "I've grown rather attached to this planet."

She waggled her tail and swam up into the sky, floating away over the rooftops of Nothington-on-Sea. As soon as she was gone the TV came back to life and Philip blinked.

He looked around then flopped back on to the sofa. "Oh, this is where it gets really exciting," he said. "Isn't it, Biskit? Biskit?"

But Biskit and Mitzy were already out of the door.

CHAPTER 3

AGENT DALEY

The Pet Defenders stepped out of the stairwell. Being such a cold blustery day, there weren't many humans around as they crossed the car park.

"So where shall we check first?" asked Mitzy.

"How about the Town Hall?"

Mitzy turned to see who had spoken. To her surprise, a scruffy red-furred fox stepped out from behind a bin.

"Daley," said Biskit.

"Agent Daley, if you don't mind," said the fox. "I took your advice and joined the agency. I'm a Pet Defender now too."

"You mean, Commander F actually allowed a well-known alien smuggler to join the agency?" said Biskit. "He must be going soft."

"He practically begged me," said Daley. "He called me an asset."

"Are you sure you didn't mishear that?" asked Biskit.

"Positive," said Daley. "Remember, I'm able to sniff out portals. And a rather large one has just appeared at the Town Hall."

"Then what are we waiting for?" said Biskit. "Daley, you can show us where it is but remember who the senior agents are."

"Enough chat. Let's go," said Mitzy.

"Wait," said Agent Daley. "What are you two doing out so late? And what were you talking about just now?"

"Nothing," lied Mitzy.

Daley smiled. "I've spent enough of my life keeping secrets to know when there's something going on. You've got a lead, haven't you?"

"The only lead I have is hanging by Philip's front door," said Biskit.

"Very funny," said Daley. "Is it something to do with those flying noses that follow you everywhere?"

"What flying noses?" asked Mitzy.

"Those ones in that tree over there," said Daley.

The Pet Defenders peered up at the tree and spotted something glinting in the moonlight. They moved towards it and saw a large metallic nose with a camera on the end, hovering in the branches.

"Nose-bots," said Biskit. "We picked them up on Planet Bogey. Hey, we picked noses. That's funny."

"Really? Because I'm not laughing," crackled the familiar gruff tones of Commander F as the grumpy bunny's voice came out of a speaker attached to a seagull's leg.

"Now, there's a surprise," said Biskit.

"Less of your cheek. You two have broken the Pet Defenders' first and most important rule. You have allowed aliens on to our planet. It was your idea that the Snot Snatchers filmed your activities and now you have jeopardized our entire organization by broadcasting everything we do across the known universe."

By the end of his speech, the commander was yelling so loudly that his words were distorted and hard to hear. Then he dropped his voice down to a low whisper and said, "From now on, Daley's going to keep an eye on you."

"Daley keep an eye on us?" said Biskit, glancing at the fox. "He used to smuggle aliens!"

"Good point, Agent Biskit. You'd better keep an eye on him, too," said the commander. "I don't trust him either."

Mitzy gave Biskit a quizzical look. "So you want us to watch him and him to watch us?" she said.

"Yes. And I'll keep an eye on me," said Commander F.

Biskit, Mitzy and Daley exchanged a glance.

"Er, you don't trust yourself?" said Biskit.

"No I do not," said the grouchy rabbit. "After that business with the shape-shifting Atomic Burps I always give myself a good hard stare in the mirror in the morning, you know, to check that it really is me. Now, all three of you, get to work."

CHAPTER 4

❖

FAME AT LAST

The Pet Defenders paused before stepping into the town square. Mitzy took cover under a bench. Biskit and Daley joined her.

"It's deserted," said Daley. "What are we hiding from?"

"Oh, there's always something to hide from," said Biskit.

"And someone," said Mitzy, edging further under the bench as a bicycle whizzed past. "You need to keep your eyes and ears open. Being a Pet Defender isn't just about protecting the planet. It's about protecting the humans."

One the bike had gone, she stepped out. Daley followed her.

"Protecting them from what? The truth?" said Daley.

"Yes," said Mitzy. "Our seagulls have to drop Forget-Me-Plop on any human who sees anything out of the ordinary."

"And a fox, dog and cat taking a trip to the Town Hall isn't exactly what they expect to see on an average Tuesday," said Biskit. "Now, stop asking questions." He led the others to a circular fountain, using its low wall to stay out of sight of any potential witnesses in the windows of the buildings that overlooked the square.

"I'd be more worried about those nose-bots, if I were you," said Daley, waving his tail at one of the alien cameras hovering high up in a tree.

"I think they're getting less cautious about being seen," said Mitzy.

"Never mind them," said Biskit, scampering up the steps of the Town Hall. "Where's the portal?"

"Right in front of you," said Daley.

"That's not a portal," said Mitzy. "That's a door."

"The portal must be on the other side," said Biskit, jumping up at the handle only for Daley to grab hold of his tail and bring him down with a **THFLUMP!**

Biskit spun round angrily. "What did you do that for?"

"Look," said Daley. "Look at it!"

Biskit peered closely at the door. As he looked at the detail of the wooden panels and the flaky paint, he noticed the whole thing shimmer.

"The door is the portal," said Mitzy, her eyes widening.

"Exactly," said Daley. "One more step and you'd have been lost on the other side of the universe. It's lucky I was here to stop you."

"Yeah well, I prefer windows to doors." Biskit ran round the side of the building then jumped up on to a window ledge.

"Biskit," said Mitzy. "Stop showing off. We need to be careful."

"Sorry. Careful isn't really my thing," said Biskit. He pushed open the window and entered the building.

It was dark inside the Town Hall so Biskit

couldn't tell what he had landed on. It was soft like a luxurious carpet except, when he tried to lift his paws, he found that all four of them were stuck.

Mitzy and Daley appeared at the window.

"Are you all right, Biskit?" said Mitzy, peering into the darkness.

"Stay where you are," said Biskit.

The lights flickered on and Biskit saw that his paws were caught in thick strands of sticky webbing that covered the ground. And in the centre of the web was a huge, hairy-legged spider.

Mitzy and Biskit recognized her at once. The eight long hairy limbs and wild devilish eyes were unmistakable. On her head she wore a yellow visor. She let out a high-pitched cackle.

"Annascratch," whispered Biskit.

"And she's got the Relativisor," said Mitzy.

"What are you two talking about?" asked Daley. "Who's Annascratch?"

"I'm Annascratch," said the huge hairy spider. "And I'm here to scratch your little planet off the map, Biskit and Mitzy."

Daley turned to look at them. "She knows you too?"

"Er, apparently so," said Mitzy.

"Oh, everyone knows you," said Annascratch. "The nose-bots broadcast your adventures across the galaxy. The show's a hit. I never miss an episode."

"So are you saying we're famous?" said Biskit, his eyes lighting up with wonder.

"Oh yes, you've got quite a following in the dimmer star systems," said Annascratch.

"Hey, you can say what you like about me but don't insult my fans," said Biskit, noticing that the nose-bot was hovering outside the window filming the whole thing.

"Yes, how devastated they'll be when the show gets cancelled due to unforeseen circumstances." Annascratch laughed hysterically.

"I don't get it. Why do villains always laugh like that?" asked Biskit. "I don't see what's so funny."

"Then let me explain the joke," said Annascratch. "With this Relativisor, I'm going to take control of the universe and there's nothing you or anyone else can do to stop me." She cackled crazily.

"It's still not actually a joke, is it?" said Mitzy.

"OK. What about this one? What did the

Tarangutan with the Relativisor say to the dog before shrinking him down to the size of a speck of dust?" She scuttled forwards, her eyes focusing on Biskit.

"Er, something about feeling small?" Biskit struggled to free himself from the web, managing to pull one paw off it before realizing he had nowhere to put it down.

"Biskit, reach for my paw," said Mitzy.

"Oh yes," said Annascratch. "Agent Mitzy tries to rescue her brave but foolish partner. Classic stuff. Except that you won't be making any jokes at the end of this episode."

Annascratch raised one of her hairy limbs and flicked a switch on the Relativisor. A yellow laser beam fired at Biskit, meaning Mitzy had to make a split-second decision. Unable to pull him to safety, she did the only thing she could to save her partner. She threw herself forwards so the beam hit her instead.

FLA-WHASSH-ZOP!

Mitzy vanished.

"Mitzy!" barked Biskit.

"And now it's your turn." Annascratch took aim with the Relativisor again. Biskit tried to free his feet. It was hopeless. "You won't win," he said, through his gritted teeth.

"I do see that it seems a little early in your adventure to meet your end," said Annascratch. "We've not even had the first commercial break yet. Oh well. Never mind." She was about to activate the Relativisor again when something red and furry landed on top of her.

Biskit saw that Daley had found another window and jumped on Annascratch in the nick of time.

"Get off," yelled the spider, throwing her arms up and her head back so that the laser beam from her visor missed Biskit but connected with the web instead. It shrank down to nothing, releasing him.

Annascratch tipped her head forwards, shaking off Daley. As he flew through the air, he grabbed the Relativisor between his jaws, then landed into a roll before springing back to his feet. Annascratch fired a web and retrieved the visor from him but Daley and Biskit were now approaching.

"Bring back my partner," said Biskit.

"Careful," said Annascratch. "For all I know, you've just stepped on her."

"There's nowhere to run to," said Biskit.

"You couldn't be more wrong. I've got everywhere to run to." Annascratch laughed again, then scuttled across the room and vanished into the rippling portal.

Daley turned to Biskit. "She got away," he said.

"I don't care about her. We need to help

Mitzy," said Biskit. "Mitzy? Can you hear me?"

"We can't do anything without that Relativisor," said Daley.

"You're right. In which case, we need to follow her," said Biskit.

"Through the portal?" said Daley, with a nervous gulp.

"Yes, through the portal," replied Biskit, scratching an itch on his head.

"But it could lead to anywhere in the universe," said Daley.

"I'd go a lot further than that to save my partner. You can stay here if you want, but I'm going through that portal."

"Oh all right, but if we end up on a planet with poisonous air I'm blaming you," said Daley.

CHAPTER 5

THE LICE SQUAD

Mitzy was lost and alone in a strange world. She had no idea how she'd got there or how to find her way back. The ground shuddered beneath her paws. She extended her claws and dug them into the pink rubbery surface, then looked up at the huge leafless trees that swayed over her head.

"Biskit!" she yelled.

"**MMMMMMMOTCH-ZEEEEE...**" rumbled the ground.

Mitzy tried to steady her breathing to calm

herself down. She needed to think. She raised a leg to clean it. The act of cleaning always helped her think straight.

She had to work out where she was. She looked up at the strange tree trunks. They didn't have branches and they were so tall that many of their tops flopped back down with their own weight. The ground beneath her feet was soft and squidgy. But the thing that was most overpowering was the smell. It wasn't totally unfamiliar but it was extremely strong. The ground trembled again and she heard a noise ten times deeper than a foghorn.

"**MMMMMMOOOOTCH-ZEEEEE...**"

Another earthquake knocked her off her feet. Wherever she was, it was unstable. Mitzy slid along the ground and collided with one of the tree trunks. **BOINGG!** She bounced off it, as though it was made of rubber. To steady herself, she sank her claws into the ground.

The sky darkened as a huge shadow fell over her. Then something came crashing towards her, parting the trees. It looked like an upside-down mountain falling from the sky. A huge claw on its end scraped across the ground, leaving it red raw. Then it went back up where it had come from.

While the thundering earthquakes continued, Mitzy examined the patch of ground that had taken the brunt of the attack of the huge claw. It was deep pink. It reminded Mitzy of a scratched piece of skin.

Skin, she thought.

That's exactly what it was.

This wasn't another planet. The smell confirmed it. It was Biskit's scent. Mitzy was on Biskit's head. The trees were his hairs. The low rumbling sounds were his barks as he called her. The claw had been him scratching himself.

"BISKIT?" she yelled. There was no way
he could hear her. She had been shrunk to
the size of a speck of dust. Her voice was too
quiet. Mitzy looked around, trying to work out
where she was.

She knew her best chance of being heard
was to find her way to Biskit's ear. She drew
her claws and jumped up on to one of his

hairs. She hitched her way up, higher and higher, until she could make out the tops of the other hairs. From this position she could see his gigantic ear, rising up on the horizon.

Large colourful shapes shifted in the hazy sky. Whatever Biskit was doing, it was making Mitzy feel as sick as a dog. Or rather, she felt as sick as a cat *on* a dog. At least she was certain of one thing – Biskit was still alive. His breathing was the cause of the regular earthquakes.

Unable to hold on to the top of the hair, Mitzy dropped down and dug her claws into the ground. But Biskit must have felt it because his paw came crashing down again. Mitzy rolled out of the way to avoid being scratched off his head and flung into the unknown.

She jumped to her feet and saw that she now stood in a clearing. She was still catching her breath when she heard something approaching. Whatever it was, it was moving fast, pushing aside the strands of Biskit's hair. Mitzy tried to move out of its path but it was too hard to predict which way it was heading. When it stepped into the clearing, she saw the reason.

Its six legs, two antennae and pair of large shiny eyes gave it the appearance of a flea, except for the fact that it was wearing a feather boa and an extremely fancy-looking hat.

"Oh, look at you, you *are* adorable," said the insect.

"Er, thank you?" said Mitzy hesitantly. "I'm Sabrina Nit, charmed to meet you."

She extended one of her limbs. Mitzy

was unsure what to make of her but, from the movement of the surrounding hairs, she realized that this nit wasn't alone.

"Uh oh," said Sabrina. "That's the Lice Squad. They're such drags."

Three more nits appeared out of Biskit's overgrown forest of hairs.

"Ha. There you are, Sabrina, you splitter," said the first of the nits.

They were all the same size, but unlike Sabrina they had used Biskit's hair to fashion whips, truncheons and helmets.

"Mina, Nina, Trina," said Sabrina. "Look at this darling little creature."

"You're a disgrace to the Squad," said Nina.

"And to the whole army," said Trina.

"You'd better fall into line now," said Mina, cracking her whip.

"Oh, come on. Don't be so uptight," said Sabrina. "All you do is march back and forth, training. I don't want to march. I want to conga. Come on, join in."

She bent over and danced along, kicking her legs out, but the others just stared at her.

"What are you doing on my partner's head?" asked Mitzy.

"I think it's a kind of rumba," said Sabrina.

"You're an embarrassment, Sabrina." Mina turned to Mitzy. "She hasn't been right in the head ever since her programming."

"What programming?" said Mitzy.

"All of Annascratch's nits receive intensive

brain-training to make sure we are loyal and determined," said Mina. "Something happened to Sabrina during the process."

"Oh yes. It was wonderful, like my eyes were suddenly opened," interrupted Sabrina, throwing her feather boa over Nina.

Mina sliced straight through it with a claw, not bothering to hide her irritation. "As you can see, she's gone wrong."

"You mean, gone right," said Sabrina dreamily. "Yes, I knew that I had to get away from the Lice Squad and do my own thing."

"Well, now you're coming back with us," said Trina.

"Yes, the invasion is imminent," added Nina.

"Quiet," said Mina. "While we're stuck on this filthy flea-bag, let me do the talking."

"Hey, if anyone's going to call my partner a filthy flea-bag it's me," said Mitzy, glancing around at the lumps of food and other bits and pieces in Biskit's hair.

Sabrina picked up a lump of dandruff and sculpted it into the shape of a flower.

"It's a dandruff dandelion," she said, attaching the flower to her hat.

"Stop messing around, Sabrina," said Mina, snatching the flower and throwing it away.

"You're not my boss," said Sabrina.

"Of course I am," snapped Mina. "Don't forget, Annascratch made me Major Mina. Whereas you are only a minor, Sabrina. Nina and Trina, help us arrest this enemy agent."

The three nits brandished their weapons at Mitzy.

"Oh, look at that," said Mitzy, pointing over their shoulders with her tail. "A nit comb."

"What?"

All three spun round, only to find that there was nothing behind them. When they turned back, Mitzy was gone.

CHAPTER 6

PORTAL LOOP TRAP

As a Pet Defenders agent, Biskit had sent
countless numbers of aliens through portals
as well as losing his previous partner in one.
But he had never stepped through one before
himself. It was a sensation like no other. If
pushed to describe it, he would have said
that it felt like being skewered by a unicorn's
horn then cooked in a microwave. But the
pain vanished as quickly as it arrived and Biskit
dropped out the other side, landing on a
planet with purple skies and yellow trees.

Daley was right behind him and they both splashed down into a pool of water.

"Wow, what a rush," said Daley.

"Er, I don't think it's stopped," said Biskit.

The water had formed a whirlpool that pulled them down into another portal. After the same painful sensation, they dropped into a different planet, where everything was green and gunky. They barely had time to understand what they were looking at before they fell through yet another portal. And another. Each one revealing a different planet, stranger than the one before.

"What's going on?" asked Daley.

"You've stepped into some kind of portal vortex," said a familiar voice that appeared to be coming from Daley's tail.

"Why is your tail talking?" asked Biskit.

"I've no idea," said Daley, swishing it around as they fell.

"Ha, no," said the voice. "It is I, Example One, of the Nothington Extraterrestrial Research Division. I'm speaking through a tracking communicator attached to Agent Daley's tail."

Biskit and Daley tumbled past a planet populated entirely by sausages wearing scarves.

"It's quite a clever little trap this," continued Example One. "You see, by creating two portals, one positioned above the other, the gravitational pull of every planet you arrive on ensures that there is no escape."

"Great," said Biskit. "But can you stop it?"

"Yes, I should imagine so," said Example
One. "It's simply a matter of switching the end
location in one of the portals to Earth and
then closing the loop."

Biskit and Daley were falling through a
brightly coloured cloud of gas. A giant moth
narrowly missed them as they yet again fell into
another portal.

"Would you mind getting on with it?" yelled Biskit. "Because I'm feeling sick and I've no interest in seeing all that popcorn again."

"Yes, of course," said Example One. "Just a moment. Now, brace yourselves."

The next portal they fell through brought them on to a planet with a comfortingly familiar sky. They were back on Earth, high in the sky. Biskit realized they were heading towards Nothington-on-Sea's rubbish dump but as they dropped, they could see there was still another portal below them. Biskit tried to change direction by wagging his tail to avoid it. They were falling fast and he feared they would soon be on the other side of the universe.

"Example One!" yelled Biskit.

Biskit and Daley hit the ground, but this time, instead of falling through another portal, they came into sharp contact with an old ironing board lying on a pile of rubbish.

"Ow," said Daley, rubbing his head with his paw.

"Thanks," said Biskit, checking that nothing was broken.

Next to them, a bespectacled pink mouse sat on the back of a seagull.

Example One pulled a chip from his holster, fed it to the seagull and hopped off. "Think nothing of it," he said. "Where's Mitzy?"

"She's been shrunk," said Biskit.

"Shrunk?"

"Annascratch hit her with a Relativisor," said Daley.

"Oh really? How interesting." Example One adjusted his glasses. "I've been playing around with a similar device myself."

"Does that mean you can help her?" demanded Biskit.

"Yes, I believe I can. It would be a matter of returning the molecules to their original size. I would have to know where she was though. Any ideas?"

Biskit had stopped listening. There was a much softer voice talking in his ear. It was quieter than a pin landing on a cushion but he recognized it at once.

"Biskit. Can you hear me?" said the voice.

"Mitzy?" said Biskit.

"What?" asked Example One, confused.

"We don't know where she is," said Daley.

"She's in my ear," said Biskit.

CHAPTER 7

☙

NITS AND PIECES

Mitzy was running across the top of Biskit's head where the hairs were thicker, making the forest of follicles denser and darker. It became harder to avoid the boulders of dandruff and dirt but she stumbled on as fast as she could. She knew that the Lice Squad was close behind. She could hear them goading her and arguing among themselves.

"Stop in the name of the Lice Squad," ordered Mina.

"Yeah, we're an itch you can't scratch,"

added Nina.

"Not even with a special shampoo," said Trina.

"Shampoo?" said Sabrina. "What a lovely sounding word. Shampoo doodle doodle dee do…"

"Stop that noise," yelled Mina.

"You call it noise," said Sabrina. "I call it music."

When at last Mitzy reached the ear, she had to scramble down the steep cliffside of Biskit's head to reach the huge cavernous opening. She crawled on to the ledge, through a thicket of hair and into his ear.

"Biskit! Can you hear me?" she yelled.

"Me… Me… Me…" Her voice echoed off the walls.

"**MOOOOTCH-ZZTEEEEE?**" came his thundering reply.

"I'm inside your ear," shouted Mitzy.

"**SHEEEE'S INNNN MY EAAAAAAAAAR!!!!**" boomed Biskit.

It was so loud that Mitzy was jamming her paws into her ears to block out the noise when the nits pushed aside the tufty hedge and entered.

"There she is," said Mina.

"She-is… She-is… She-is…" repeated the echo.

"Oo, great acoustics," said Sabrina, twirling around and slipping an elbow-length glove over one hand then singing, "La-la-la… Me-me-me…"

"Me… me… me…" echoed her voice.

"This is not about you, you or you," snarled Mina. "You are a part of the Lice Squad. You're supposed to be a trained soldier."

"I'm no solider. I'm a soul-diva," said Sabrina, again bursting into song. "Biddly-doodly-day…"

"Stop doing that!" snapped Mina. "And stop accessorizing."

"Izing… Izing… Izing…"

"**WHEEEN I SAY LEET GO, LEET GO**," came Biskit's Earth-shaking voice.

"I'm ready," said Mitzy.

"What is that sound?" asked Trina.

"That's my partner," said Mitzy.

Suddenly, the ground beneath their feet dramatically tilted. Biskit's massive ear flopped open as he tipped his head on its side. For Mitzy this felt as though the whole world was flipping upside down.

"**NOOOOWWWW!**" sounded Biskit's

voice like a ship's foghorn.

She let go and fell backwards, her legs flailing.

"Lice Squad. After her," yelled Mina.

Biskit peered down at the swirling dust, but he couldn't tell if Mitzy was there or not.

"OK, stand back," said Example One, moving the stylus over the screen of his small electronic tablet. "You see, it's really just a matter of relativity. Mitzy is only small in relation to us. We simply need to reverse the effects of the Relativisor and ... hey presto."

A yellow beam fired out of Example One's tablet. There was a **FLASH!** and a **CRACK!** and a **FLASH-ba-da-KRACK!** as the beam split into five strands and produced four insects piled up on top of each other. Underneath their large bottoms was one rather squashed-looking cat.

"Mitzy," said Biskit.

"Hey, Biskit," mumbled
Mitzy. "I've got nits."

"Get off her," barked Biskit.

The nits rolled out of each other's way and
Mitzy stood up tentatively.

"How did we end up here?" asked Mitzy,

checking that nothing was broken.

"We took a long cut across the universe," said Daley. "Still, it was worth the trip to end up in this stinky old rubbish dump," he added sarcastically.

"Hey, what was it like on my head?" asked Biskit.

"I don't want to talk about it." Mitzy shuddered. "But next time Philip runs you a bath, I'm helping him force you into it. There are things in your fur that I never want to see again."

"Is that where you found this lot?" asked Daley.

"This is the Lice Squad," said Mitzy.

"Yes," said Mina. "A special division of Annascratch's secret army, designed to protect our glorious leader during the invasion."

"The invasion? Is that now?" asked Nina, scratching her head.

"We've been expanded. It must be," said

66

Trina, smashing up a broken toaster, stretching the metal and twisting it into the shape of a crossbow.

"About time," said Nina, grabbing a can and pulling it into the shape of an arrow.

"We'd better make sure we look our best then." Sabrina picked up a roll of wire and fashioned a new feather boa.

"You're such a loser, Sabrina," said Nina.

"Looking good isn't a crime," said Sabrina, finding a big floppy discarded hat and placing it on her head. "But if it was, I'd plead guilty."

"Stop arguing, all of you," said Mina. "Now, arm yourselves and prepare to fight."

The nits were extremely quick at making weapons. In a matter of seconds, Mina, Nina and Trina were pointing all kinds of destructive devices at the Pet Defenders. Sabrina, however, was busily adding sparkly things to the hat she had found.

Biskit, Daley and Mitzy backed away to where Example One was climbing on to his seagull.

"Can't you reverse the effect and shrink them back down?" asked Biskit.

"Given time, I suppose so…" began Example One, tinkering with his tablet while trying to steady his bird.

"We don't *have* time," said Biskit.

"What about Forget-Me-Plop?" said Mitzy. "That should slow them down."

"Excellent suggestion," said Example One.

He typed something into his tablet and four seagulls swooped down from nearby rooftops, dropping four loads of Forget-Me-Plop on to the nits' heads.

Mina, Nina and Trina paused to look up at the white gunk on their heads. Sabrina discarded the hat she had just made and went in search of another.

"It hasn't worked," said Daley.

"No. Your usual defences will not work on us," said Mina. "We are designed to withstand any attacks – chemical, biological or physical."

Nina fired a perfectly aimed arrow from her makeshift crossbow and knocked the tablet out of Example One's paws. It crashed to the floor in a blaze of sparks that showered out and briefly brought to life a pile of old radios and televisions.

"… now over to Carol with the weather…"

"… Southampton nil, Coventry City nil…"

"… frightening images coming in from Nothington-on-Sea—"

As the sparks vanished, the electrical devices were drained of power and fell silent once more.

"Example One, get out of here," said Mitzy, patting the seagull's behind so that it took to the air and carried the mouse to safety.

"What about the rest of us?" asked Daley.

Trina took a swing with a club made from mangled oil cans. It **KRA-RUNCHED** into the ground next to the fox, sending bits of debris flying everywhere.

"We need to find a way to stop these things." Biskit dived to avoid being sliced by a sharp-edged blade that Nina had made from a sheet of metal.

ZINNG!

"They must have a weakness." Mitzy hopped into the air to avoid rapid-fire darts from the device Mina had created from various bits of junk.

RATA-TA-BA-SPLAT!

"Lice Squad," said Mina, "we must go to the meeting point to keep our leader from danger. The invasion has begun."

"What invasion?" asked Mitzy.

"The Invasion of the Giant Nits," said Trina.

CHAPTER 8

EVEN GIANTER NITS

"What's that noise?" asked Daley.

The air was suddenly full of the sounds of cars starting and people screaming. The humans of Nothington-on-Sea were panicking.

"Follow me," said Mina, and she led the other nits out of the rubbish dump and down towards the centre of town.

"Phew," sighed Daley. "At least they've gone."

"We need to follow them," said Mitzy.

"What?" said Daley.

"She's right," said Biskit. "This town has a nit

problem and we need to comb the area and wash them away."

Biskit, Mitzy and Daley took after the nits but it was hard to keep up. The streets were full of humans running in the opposite direction. Seagulls were dive-bombing with Forget-Me-Plop but they had their work cut out with so many moving targets.

The Pet Defenders turned the corner into Town Hall Square, where they saw Annascratch standing in front of the fountain surrounded by giant nits tearing up the place.

The spider carefully shook one of her hairy legs then fired her Relativisor at her tiny army. As the yellow light of the laser beam fizzled away, more freshly grown nits sprang up and set about arming themselves.

The Lice Squad took their place in front of Annascratch, each holding an assortment of improvised weapons.

"And so it all begins," said Annascratch, looking up at the nose-bots and speaking directly into the camera. "Today we will conquer this world, then from here we will seize control of the entire universe." She threw back her head and fired the Relativisor.

"NITS... NITS... NITS..." cried Mina.

"ITCH... ITCH... ITCH..." responded the ever-growing army.

"ANNA... ANNA... ANNA..." yelled Mina.

"SCRATCH... SCRATCH... SCRATCH..." hollered the rest.

Annascratch cackled.

"Again, with that laugh," said Mitzy.

"I'll wipe that smile off her face," said Biskit.

He went to move but Mitzy sat on his tail and held him back. "No, Biskit. Last time she shrank me and sent you tumbling across the universe. Before we do anything, we need a plan."

"We have to stop her growing more of her nits," said Biskit, pulling his tail free.

"Then we need that Relativisor," said Daley. "How can we get it off her if we can't get near her?"

"It's time to ask for help." Mitzy lowered her head to press the button on her pendant but Biskit shook his head.

"No. We can do this." He turned and ran across the square. He weaved his way through the giant nits, expertly dodging every attack. He was so fast that Annascratch didn't see him until it was too late.

Biskit pounced, catching her off-guard while she was halfway through firing at more miniscule nits shaken from her hairy legs. So she tilted her head back and the laser beam hit a row of soldiers that were already full size.

Mitzy and Daley watched in horror as nits the size of humans grew until they were bigger than houses.

"Uh oh!" Mitzy gulped. "It looks like our nit problem just got bigger."

"I thought nits were the eggs," said Daley. "Aren't these lice?"

"Now is not the time for nit-picking," said Mitzy. "Biskit's in trouble. Look!"

Annascratch fired a web at him. It encircled Biskit and wrapped him up like a mummy.

"You won't hold me," said Biskit, rolling away and tripping up several nits, but he was unable to free himself.

"Oh, I know you *think* that, Agent Biskit," said Annascratch, adjusting the Relativisor and moving closer. "I've watched your show enough times to know that you always save the day. So what a twist it will be this time when you don't."

"The baddie wins?" said Biskit. "Interesting idea but I don't think anyone will buy it."

"How about an ending in which I rescue my partner, then we send you and your nits packing?" said Mitzy, stepping out into the open.

"Too predictable," said Annascratch, firing a web at Mitzy.

Mitzy dived out of the way, but the giant nits were more alert this time. One swung an electrocuting truncheon made from a traffic light. **ZZiiPinG!** Mitzy leaped out of the way but landed in front of another nit. This one had a net made out of iron railings. Mitzy ducked and rolled to avoid it but the net was too big and the nit was too fast. The nit scooped up Mitzy, then sealed the iron mesh shut. She jabbed her claw into Mitzy's side. Mitzy scrabbled to escape, but she was trapped.

"Daley," she yelled. "Get us out of here."

"Er, sorry, Mitzy," he said. "Annascratch has got you both. There's nothing I can do."

"Daley!" cried Mitzy, but the quick fox jumped over a bench and under the swinging arm of a giant nit and made his getaway.

"I have Biskit in knots," said Annascratch. "And Mitzy netted by a nit. Not bad. Now, I think it's time for my close-up."

Annascratch looked up at a tree and addressed the nose-bots that were hovering behind a branch. "You'll want to get a good shot for this. This is the bit where I defeat the Pet Defenders and take control of the universe."

The two nosed-shaped cameras silently drifted down from the trees.

"I'm sorry, Mitzy," said Biskit. "You were right. We needed a plan."

Annascratch hooted with evil laughter.
"Yes, Biskit, Mitzy is usually right but your
fans love your daredevil stunts anyway." She
waved at the camera. "And this show goes out
live, which is more than could be said for the
Pet Defenders. But I'll keep you around long
enough to witness the destruction of your
beloved planet."

Annascratch shook one of her legs and fired
the Relativisor again, creating yet more giant
nits. The nits quickly got to work, tearing up
whatever they could find, bending and shaping
it into a variety of sophisticated weaponry.

Mitzy caught Biskit's eye. "Ready to admit
we need help?" she said.

"Do you know what, I think I am," said
Biskit.

Mitzy lowered her head and nudged the
button on the pendant around her neck.

CHAPTER 9

A SECOND SECRET ARMY

The pendant dropped to the ground. Fearing it to be some kind of grenade, the nits backed away but Annascratch moved closer to look at it.

"What's this?" she said mockingly. "Is that SUPA technology? Did Zed give this to you when he got you to do his dirty work? Unfortunately, I know all of their tricks. I created every gadget they use. Whatever it is, it's no threat to me."

Annascratch kicked the pendant away but,

as she made contact, it suddenly exploded in a blinding flash of light. The spider staggered back. The pendant **FIZZED** and **FUZZED** and **CRACKLED** and **SIZZLED**, then a hundred laser beams fired out from it. When the lasers finished, Mitzy and Biskit saw that a collection of strange creatures had appeared out of nowhere. Countless breeds of alien from every corner of the universe were standing in the square alongside the giant nits. From the gadgets they wore and carried, Mitzy recognized them as SUPA agents.

"Oi, watch who you're pushing," said Nina, firing a dart from a blowpipe at a creature that looked like a cross between a monkey and skunk.

"Yeah, get out of it," said Trina, stabbing a large jelly-like blob with a spear. The wobbly alien just slipped away, apparently unharmed.

"Get back," said Mina, whacking another

with the roof of a bus shelter.

All the new arrivals looked different but
they wore variations of Zed's flashing collar
and tail gun. It was the most extraordinary
scene, full of wildly weird creatures, but Biskit
was staring at a distinctly more familiar face.
A shaggy-haired Old English sheepdog was
standing at the centre of the SUPA agents.

Biskit felt a dizzying mixture of emotions seeing his old partner again, but all he could manage to utter was the dog's name. "Champ?"

"Biskit." Champ wagged his tail and smiled. "It's good to see you again, old buddy. Do you need a paw with that webbing?"

"No, I'm fine," said Biskit.

Champ nudged a button on his collar and fired his tail gun at the web, freeing Biskit immediately. He laughed. "You never did like asking for help. That's why Zed and I gave the pendant to your new partner."

"You're Champ?" said Mitzy. "I thought you weren't allowed back on Earth."

"Desperate times call for desperate measures, Mitzy," said Champ. He fired a red laser beam from his tail gun at the net. It came so close to Mitzy that she could feel its heat on her bottom but it tore straight through the metal, allowing her to drop to the ground.

"Thanks," she said.

"You've saved my old partner enough times," said Champ. "I owed you. Although we should really sort out this nit problem before we have a proper catch-up."

"Senior SUPA Agent Champ." Annascratch aimed the Relativisor at him. "Do you really think you can use my own technology to ambush me?"

"It isn't your technology," replied Champ. "You were working for us when you developed it. We funded your department so your inventions could help keep the universe safe."

"It will be safe," said Annascratch. "Under my control."

"Hold on, what?" said Mitzy. "You mean, I've been carrying these agents in that pendant all this time. So when I was shrunk down to the size of a nit, they must have been the size of atoms?"

"Yep. That's about the size of it," said Champ, winking at her.

Everywhere, nits were busily constructing complicated weapons from anything they could find while the SUPA agents did their best to stop them. One of the nits twisted a lamppost and tore off car roofs to create a hand-held cannon. It aimed it at Biskit but a SUPA agent formed of blue smoke swirled around his head, making him miss.

A group of nits circled around the Pet Defenders, blocking their way to Annascratch. They faced the army of SUPA Agents, whose fingers, toes, flippers, tentacles and noses hovered over the triggers of their colourful collars.

"Come on, Annascratch," said Champ. "You've worked for us for long enough to know how this whole *mad scientist taking over the universe* thing works out. We win, you lose."

"Not this time," said Annascratch. "You don't spend that long at a crime-fighting agency without learning the formula of failure. Do you know where all those super-criminals go wrong?"

"Is it the big speeches?" said Biskit.

"Or the crazy laughs?" said Mitzy.

"No," said Champ. "They lose because they always underestimate us."

"Precisely," said Annascratch. "But I can't underestimate you because I know everything about you." She raised her head and hollered, "Giant nit army, destroy the SUPA agents!"

CHAPTER 10

ATTACK OF THE GIANT NITS

"Well?" screeched Annascratch. "What are you waiting for, permission from your mothers? Nits attack!"

"Nits… Nits… Nits," yelled Mina.

"Attack… Attack… Attack…" responded the nits.

And with that cry, they unleashed a battle like no other. Biskit and Mitzy took cover. The soldier insects fired bazookas made from bins, loaded with cannonballs made from crushed-up bottles. Others shot flaming arrows, lobbed explosives or swung electrified hammers.

The Pet Defenders and the SUPA agents took evasive action, diving, rolling and sliding out of the way. Seeing one of the enormous nits aiming its weapon at him, Champ nudged the button on his collar and shot a blue laser at it.

"Time to blitz the nits," he said.

The nit froze.

Annascratch laughed.

"What's so funny?" asked Champ.

"I designed that Stare Ray," said Annascratch. "And I bred these nits."

The frozen nit twitched.

"SUPA agents," yelled Champ. "Your Stare Rays have no effect on the nits."

"Oh, I wouldn't say that," said Annascratch.

The nit looked confused by what happened next because, in the blink of an eye, it suddenly swelled in size until it was as tall as a surrounding block of flats.

"Your weapons are worse than useless," said Annascratch. "All settings will only make my nit army bigger."

Champ gulped. "This is bad," he admitted.

More lights came on as the residents of Nothington-on-Sea drew back their curtains to gawp at the enormous nits tearing up their town.

Annascratch's army twisted metal, snapped plastic and scratched at concrete as they created more weapons and artillery from the cars, lampposts and pavements. The square was rich in materials for them to use, but the Pet Defenders could see the army was already starting to spill out into the surrounding streets.

"So this is the plan?" said Mitzy. "You're going to take control of Earth, then use it as a base for attacking the rest of the universe?"

Annascratch swung around to face her. "Oh no, my plan is bigger than that. Nit army, reveal the portal," she cried. "Break these walls and reveal the extent of our ambition."

The nits tore away the outside of the Town Hall, sending bricks flying everywhere and revealing that, behind the wall, the air shimmered and the dust swirled.

"The portal is growing!" gasped Mitzy.

"The whole building is a portal!" said Biskit.

"Yes and guess what?" said Annascratch. She turned back to the portal and fired a blast from the Relativisor directly at it. The yellow laser beam hit the patch of shifting sky and made it even bigger. "That's right, I'm going to make it so big that your entire planet will be sucked into it."

"But that would rip the Earth apart," said Champ.

"Precisely," said Annascratch.

"Not on my watch," snarled Biskit.

But as he and Mitzy stepped forwards, a wall of nits moved in between him and Annascratch, taking aim with their weapons.

"SUPA agents, we need to get to Annascratch to stop her making the portal bigger," yelled Champ.

"But our blaster rays are useless against them," said a three-armed SUPA agent fighting one of the nits.

Even when the SUPA agents did manage to disarm any of the nits, their enormous opponents simply made new weapons. All around the square, the giant nits were firing, swinging and slicing their weapons at the SUPA agents, who were forced to dodge the attacks. Biskit and Mitzy looked at each other and gulped.

Daley was weaving his way through the streets again, but this time he was running with the crowd. He had enjoyed his time as a Pet Defenders agent but he wasn't like Biskit and Mitzy. When it came down to it, he wasn't as brave as they were. He wanted to survive. And hanging around while an ever-growing army of giant nits appeared didn't seem like the best way to do that.

Daley darted out of the way of a speeding
motorbike, then ran slap-bang into a large
furious-looking white rabbit standing next to a
seagull with a pink mouse on its back.

"Commander F, Example One," said Daley.

"Agent Daley," said Example One. "You
appear to be advancing in the wrong direction."

"Er, I was coming to get help?" offered Daley.

"You were running away," said Commander F.

"So what if I was?" snapped Daley, suddenly defensive. "How are we supposed to fight an alien with superior technology and an army of specially bred soldiers? The SUPA agents' blasters only make them bigger and we're just a bunch of animals."

"A bunch of animals we may be," said Commander F. "But we are a bunch of animals with a mission to protect those who protect us."

"Protect us?" said Daley. "I'm a fox. Humans don't protect me."

"Nor me," said Example One. "In fact, quite the opposite. I was exploited and experimented on but I still work to keep this world safe. Do you know why?"

"No, why?" asked Daley.

"Because I am able to," replied Example One simply.

"And so are you," said Commander F.

"The nits are too well armed and the portal is getting too big," protested Daley.

"I can close the portal down," said Example One, "but you must stop Annascratch making it any bigger."

"We need to get the Relativisor away from her," said Commander F. "It's the only way to stop her."

"I'm sorry," said Daley, hanging his head low. "I tried, but I just don't think being brave is my thing."

"Agent Daley," snarled Commander F. "Bravery isn't anyone's *thing*. Bravery isn't something you possess. Bravery is found in one's actions. Now, turn around and get back into that fight."

"Or you could sit and wait for our planet to be destroyed if you would rather," said Example One.

"But why me?" asked Daley.

"You've spent your whole life looking out for yourself, Daley," said Commander F. "Now, it's time to help everyone else on this planet."

Three cars sped past as the human population of Nothington-on-Sea continued its mass evacuation. Daley knew Commander F was right. He had no choice. He wanted to survive but running away wasn't going to help him do that. Going back to the square wasn't just the right thing to do. It wasn't just the brave thing to do. It was the *only* thing to do.

"I've got an idea," he said.

"Good," said Commander F.

"I'll see you around," said Daley, and he sidestepped Commander F and continued running away from the Town Hall.

"Daley," yelled Commander F, but the fox didn't turn back.

CHAPTER 11

🐾

DALEY'S
DARING DEED

It wasn't the first time Mitzy and Biskit had been forced to fight for the survival of their planet, but this occasion felt more hopeless than ever. Even with the help of Champ and his SUPA agents, no one could get anywhere near Annascratch or the Relativisor.

Mina, Trina and Nina formed a protective wall around her. Sabrina was too busy making a pair of dangly earrings. Annascratch stood at the centre, firing the beam of light directly at the portal, making it larger and larger.

"I'm nearly there," said Annascratch. "The portal is almost big enough now. Feel how the fabric of reality frays."

"It's my frock fraying that I'm worried about," said Sabrina, holding down the bottom of a dress she had made out of a piece of material torn off a car seat.

"What?" asked Annascratch.

"Ignore her," said Mina. "She's a defective nit."

"Defective?" said Sabrina. "You're just jealous because I look so much better than you lot."

"No way are we jealous of you," said Trina.

"You're a disgrace," agreed Nina.

"Silence, all of you," yelled Annascratch. "Any second now, the portal will be so large it will scatter you across the known universe. Everyone will have nits! Just keep those agents away from me while I complete our work."

The nits turned back to see the Pet

Defenders creeping closer. All around them, a hundred battles raged. SUPA agents fought nits, while any humans who hadn't already fled the area ran screaming.

As Annascratch's yellow beam connected with the portal, Mitzy felt the pavement shake. But it wasn't just the ground that shook. Cracks were appearing in the sky itself.

"Biskit," said Mitzy, "the portal is so big that it is tearing everything apart. This would be a great time for you to have one of your crazy ideas about how to save the world."

Biskit made another attempt to get near Annascratch only to be thwarted yet again by the nits. He ducked under Nina's swiping blades, rolled out of the way of Trina's hammer but Mina blocked his way with an axe made from twisted scaffolding.

"There are too many of them," said Biskit.

He and Mitzy jumped up on to the wall that surrounded the fountain. Annascratch had her head tilted upwards, firing the Relativisor at the portal. Champ joined them on the wall.

"I'm sorry," he said. "There's no way to get near her."

Just then, a red-haired fox stepped out of the portal, right under Annascratch's nose. She was too preoccupied to notice and Daley was quick to move out of sight. He snuck round behind her back.

"Hey, I know that fox," said Champ.

"It's Daley," said Biskit.

"Agent Daley," said Mitzy. "He must have found a nearby portal and come through."

"He's going after the Relativisor," said Biskit.

"We need to keep the nits' eyes on us or they'll spot him," said Mitzy.

"That, I can do." Biskit sprang up and charged, barking and snarling then leaping and twisting in mid-air. He threw his weight into Trina with such power that she staggered back and fell over, crashing into Nina who, in turn, collided with Mina.

"Get him," yelled Mina. "Protect our leader."

The nits were back on their feet in no time and Biskit led them away from Annascratch. While the nits fired everything they had at him, Mitzy watched as Daley snuck up behind

Annascratch. The fox took a couple of steps back, then paused to look at Mitzy. He smiled and winked before leaping into action. He snatched the Relativisor off Annascratch's head before she knew what was happening.

"What? No! Nit army, get that fox!"

The nits spun round but Daley had already reached the portal. He paused briefly, placing the Relativisor down and saying, "Biskit, Mitzy, it's been an honour working with you. I'll see you around."

"Oh no, you don't," cried Annascratch, firing a web that attached itself to him.

"Yes, I thought you might do that," said Daley, and he picked up the Relativisor and jumped into the portal.

"No, no, this can't be happening," yelled Annascratch. "Someone cut through this web. It's pulling me in. There's no telling where I'll end up if I fall through it now."

So many nits charged to her rescue that they all crashed into each other. Before any of them could cut through the web, Annascratch was at the mouth of the portal.

"This isn't the last of me," she cried. "I'm Annascratch and I will—"

The end of her speech was cut short as she tumbled into the unknown.

CHAPTER 12

PICKING A NOSE-BOT

Annascratch was gone but the nits were
fighting on. In her absence, Mina had taken
control of the gigantic warring insects.

"Nit army," she yelled. "Our leader will
return. We must carry on with our work
until she gets back. Create weapons, take no
prisoners, attack!"

"Attack… Attack… Attack…" responded
the nits, continuing to wreak havoc.

"Annascratch is my responsibility," said
Champ. "I could have seen the signs that she

was turning bad, but I thought I could control her. That's why I've got to go after her."

"Where has she gone?" asked Biskit.

"I've no idea, but the sooner I go, the better the chance I'll come out at the same place she did. I need to bring her in. Besides, someone has to help that fox. He just saved your planet from destruction."

"My planet?" said Biskit. "This is your planet too, Champ."

"It was once," said Champ, "but I'm not even supposed to be here. This is your planet, Biskit. And though you and Mitzy do a fine job, you need our help now."

"Your help?" said Biskit.

"Yes, you must persuade Commander F that he should work with us. You know what he's like. Everything is black and white for him. He needs to realize that not all aliens mean harm."

"I'll talk to him," said Mitzy. "I agree. We've spent too long treating everyone in the universe as a threat."

"You're a good agent, Mitzy, and a better partner to Biskit than I ever was," said Champ. "Take care of each other. Now, I'd better go."

"Good luck, Champ," said Biskit.

It was the second time Biskit had witnessed his old partner disappear into a portal but this time it was different. Biskit trusted that Champ knew what he was doing. Besides, Champ wasn't his partner any more.

"Biskit, watch it!" yelled Mitzy.

The members of the Lice Squad were moving in on them, brandishing all manner of weapons.

"Get them," ordered Mina.

Nina and Trina attacked suddenly, but Biskit ducked and they smacked into each other, while Sabrina pirouetted out of the way.

"You're such clumsy movers," said Sabrina, waving a ribbon she had made in the air. "You should be more elegant like me."

Mitzy and Biskit moved away but nowhere was safe from the crossfire of the battle. Each step brought them into contact with danger as the nits waged war and the SUPA agents tried to defend themselves.

"Sabrina's right," said Mitzy.

"What? We need them to be more elegant?" asked Biskit.

"No. We need them to be more like her," replied Mitzy.

"Why is she like that?" said Biskit.

"Apparently, something went wrong in her brain-training," said Mitzy. "If we can work out what it is then we can do the same to the rest of them. Follow me."

She led Biskit across the battlefield, while chunks of broken buildings and mashed-up cars rained down on them. Laser beams fired so close over their heads that Mitzy could smell the burning strands of fur. They dived under legs and slid over car bonnets to reach Sabrina.

"Ooh, hello again," said Sabrina. "What a dreadful mess we're making."

"What happened to you, Sabrina?" asked Mitzy. "Why aren't you like the others?"

"I've no idea," said Sabrina. "All I know is that while we were being taught battle tactics, my headset picked up the wrong channel. I think it was one of your earth channels, and I heard sounds I had never heard before. Strange, wonderful sounds like this: 'la-la-la-ba-ram-ba'." She sang and danced in a circle.

"Music," said Mitzy with a nod. "You're talking about music."

"Yes," said Sabrina dreamily. "As soon as I heard it, I knew fighting wasn't for me."

Mitzy turned to Biskit. "We need to play music so they all hear it."

"Play it on what?" said Biskit, surveying the area. "These nits are tearing up everything electrical in a mile radius. There's nothing to broadcast it."

"Oh yes there is," said Mitzy, gazing up at the seagulls circling above, sending footage back to the commander. "We can use the seagull network."

"But we'll need Example One to broadcast the signal. Where is he?"

The Pet Defenders looked around for the pink mouse but such was the extent of destruction, the trained seagulls were all keeping a safe distance, far above the largest of the giant nits.

"Up there," said Biskit. "I think I see him."

High in the sky, one of the seagulls was firing a yellow laser beam at the portal. Mitzy could just make out the pink speck on the back of the gliding bird.

"Example One is trying to shrink the portal," said Mitzy. "How can we contact him?"

"I'll do it," said Biskit.

"How?" asked Mitzy. "He's way too high."

"Just help me reach that tree and I'll get the message to him."

Mitzy had no idea what her partner was planning but there wasn't time to discuss it and she had learned to trust him. So she ran alongside Biskit, keeping him safe from the nits.

When they reached the tree, Biskit scrambled up the thick trunk. He climbed to a low branch, then sprang up to another. He didn't stop to look down. He had always hated heights but he couldn't worry about that now.

His plan was to get on to one of the nose-bots that was filming them and use it to fly up to get Example One. It had seemed like a good idea until he realized the problem. Every time he climbed, the nose-bots moved further away in order to get a better view of him.

"Mitzy," he yelled down. "I need you to run towards the Town Hall. The nose-bot will follow you."

Mitzy hesitated.

"Biskit, you'll break your legs if you fall from there."

"I'd better not fall then," he replied.

It was the kind of plan that would one day get him killed. But it was also the kind of plan that only Biskit could pull off.

"Now," he yelled.

Mitzy ran towards the Town Hall.

CHAPTER 13

A CATCHY TUNE

The nose-bot suddenly swooped down to follow Mitzy, allowing Biskit to make the jump. He spread his legs wide as he glided through the air. With precision timing, he closed his paws around the top of the nose-bot. The whole thing rocked with the impact but Biskit clung on for dear life.

The nose-bot spun in circles, trying to shake him off but Biskit swished his tail and tightened his grip. He got the protruding camera between his jaws and twisted it upwards.

"Listen, Snot Snatchers," snarled Biskit, through gritted teeth. "I know you can hear me and you've had your fun. Now you need to help me."

"Nose-bots observe," said a flat electronic voice from the device. "We do not get involved."

"Involved?" Biskit twisted the camera round to point at the nits. "We need to broadcast something across our seagull network to defeat Annascratch's army ... otherwise there won't be anything to observe. No Pet Defenders, no Earth, no universe..."

"We must not intervene," said the nose-bot.

"...and no show," said Biskit.

"No show?" repeated the nose-bot. "No viewers, no adverts, no money." It paused for a moment to process this, then said, "We will help. We can broadcast on your primitive radio waves. What would you like to play?"

"Something catchy," said Biskit. "Hold on
… adverts. That's it. Find an Earth TV channel
and get ready to play it as loudly as possible.
It's Yapp Snax time."

Down below, Mitzy was busily avoiding a ball
and chain that Nina was swinging at her. As
the huge chunk of metal crunched into the
pavement, Mitzy dived behind an upside-down
bench and rolled into something soft, white
and fluffy.

"Commander F," she said. "Are you all right?"

"Oh yes, I'm just dandy," said Commander F sarcastically. "Our home town is being torn apart by giant alien nits. What could possibly be the problem?"

"We've got a plan," replied Mitzy.

"A plan?" snapped Commander F. "The entire town is in panic. It's made the news. We'll never keep this one under wraps. And I'm holding you two to blame. You brought all these aliens here in that pendant. I watched the whole thing on our seagull network. You broke our first rule. We defend the Earth from aliens. We do not invite them in."

"You're wrong, sir. The SUPA agents are helping us," said Mitzy.

As one of their red laser beams hit the bench, causing it to explode, Mitzy and Commander F rolled out of the way. Debris rained down on them.

"Oh yes, I can see that," said Commander F.

"Our planet is too small for us to work alone," said Mitzy. "Sometimes you have to know when to ask for help."

Whatever Commander F had to say was lost as a crushed motorbike came crashing down between them.

SMAKURRANCSHHHH!

As the motorbike's wheels rolled away, a new sound filled the air. An orchestra was playing. Mitzy recognized the music before the choir of voices belted out the words.

"Give your dogs and cats a treat,
With Yapp Snax every day to eat
Our tasty bites are just sublime
They're fabulous and SO divine."

She caught Commander F's eye but he was too astonished to speak. One by one the nits

stopped attacking. They lowered their guns
and dropped their blades. They shook off their
armour and raised their heads. They listened.
Only one nit moved. Sabrina spun round
and round, dancing to the music and crying,
"Wonderful. Isn't it wonderful?"

"What's happening?" asked Commander F.

"They're being reprogrammed," said Mitzy.

"What is this noise?" asked Mina.

"It's called music," said Mitzy. "This one gets
stuck in your head. Just like you nits, really."

"Nits?" said Sabrina, with a snazzy little side-shuffle. "We aren't nits. We're fabu-louse."

"I just want to dance," said Nina, twirling around.

"Make music not war," said Trina, picking up a car exhaust, poking holes in it and turning it into a flute.

"I'm a diva not a destroyer," said Mina, adding a flamboyant collar to her battle dress.

Biskit landed next to Mitzy with a **FLUTHUMP!** "Now we just need to get them off the planet before the portal vanishes."

"I've got an idea," said Mitzy. "Hey, Sabrina. Maybe it's time to try a conga again?"

"In that direction," said Biskit, pointing towards the portal.

"Wonderful idea," said Sabrina. "Come on, everyone, follow me. We're taking this show on the road."

CHAPTER 14

❧

A NEW BEGINNING

Commander F stared in utter bewilderment as the last of the giant nits danced through the portal. Example One brought his seagull down and fired a final laser beam at it, sealing it up.

"Of course, I'll have to check all the other portals that may have appeared in town," said Example One, "but this one is safe again."

All around the square, the SUPA agents were busily using the Unmistaker settings on their ray guns to repair the damage. Buildings put themselves back together, cars uncrushed their bonnets and bins leaped back into place.

"It's such remarkable technology," said Example One.

"And being used in plain sight of human witnesses," said Commander F. "We need to get wiping memories."

Biskit and Mitzy joined them.

"There isn't enough Forget-Me-Plop in the world," said Biskit. "We can't contain this."

"Yes. It's time for the truth to come out," said Mitzy, "about everything, including us."

"The truth?" said Commander F. "Have you lost your mind, Agent Mitzy? Humans won't be able to deal with that."

"I'm sorry, Commander F," said Mitzy, "but I think you're wrong."

"How dare you?" he blustered. "Example One, talk some sense into her, will you?"

"Actually, sir," said Example One, "I think Mitzy may be right. The only course of action left to us is to allow the humans to learn the truth."

"But… But…" began Commander F. "They're not ready."

"Is anyone ever ready to discover that their planet is the central invading point of the entire universe?" asked Mitzy.

"I wasn't," said Biskit.

"And nor were you, Fluffikins, when I made first contact," said a female voice.

A bulbous-eyed goldfish in a floating sphere of water appeared out of nowhere. "It is time," said Barb. "You've protected your owners for so long. Now you have to trust them. Maybe this knowledge will be the thing that unites them. Knowing that they are just a small part of an infinite universe has to change something. I think, with your guidance, your owners could manage it. And I have a vastly superior understanding of things compared to you."

"Modest as ever," said Biskit.

"Am I the only one who thinks this a terrible idea?" demanded Commander F.

"You don't have a choice," said Barb. "Whether you accept it or not, you can't stop word getting out now."

"But … but everything will change," said Commander F, sounding utterly dismayed.

"Everything is always changing," said Mitzy. "The trick is to make sure that it's changing for the better."

Commander F shook his head, unconvinced but aware that he was alone in his opinion. "In which case I will have to change too."

"What?" Mitzy and Biskit spoke together.

"My job as commander of the Pet Defenders has been to ensure not just the safety of our planet but the secrecy of our organization. If our secrets are going to come out then my dear owner, Emily, will never see me in the same way again. In her eyes, I am a sweet fluffy rabbit. I'd like to stay being that to her. She's more important to me than… Well, anyone."

"I don't understand. What are you saying, sir?" asked Mitzy.

"I'm stepping down," said Commander F. "Well, hopping down, I suppose." He chuckled. "I'm retiring. I'm going back to being Emily's rabbit. I'm going back to being Fluffikins."

"But who will take your place?" asked Biskit.

"Someone who is ready to take on a new challenge which will see humans, pets and aliens working together," said Commander F.

"Example One?" said Mitzy.

"I'm no leader," said the pink mouse.

"Then who?" asked Biskit.

"If it were my decision, I'd give your partner the job, Biskit," said Commander F. "She's smart, calm under pressure and one of the bravest agents I know. Besides, if she can keep you alive, she can certainly be trusted to keep our planet safe. Good luck, Pet Defenders."

The large white rabbit turned and hopped away.

Biskit turned to Mitzy. "Commander M?" he said.

Mitzy let out a small, embarrassed meow. "I'm not a commander."

"Yes you are," said Biskit firmly. "We need you. You figured out how to save us from the nits and it wasn't the first time. You've saved the planet many times and you saved me."

"You?"

Biskit nodded. "When I first met you, I didn't think I wanted a partner. Losing Champ had hit me pretty hard. You showed me that we're stronger when we work as a team."

"You'll still be my partner," said Mitzy. "That won't change."

"If you insist," said Biskit, grinning from ear to ear.

"But we need to work with Zed's SUPA agency from now on," said Mitzy. "Our planet is too small not to need help occasionally."

"Well said," agreed Example One, patting his seagull's head. "I say, where's Daley?"

"Somewhere out there," said Mitzy, looking up at the stars. "He did a very brave thing."

"Yes, he came good in the end," said Biskit. "So what now, Commander M?"

Mitzy paused to clean her back leg, removing the bits of dust and dirt she had picked up during the battle.

"We're Pet Defenders, Biskit," she replied. "Only now, it's not just the Earth we're defending. It's the whole universe."